W9-BLS-361

DUCK
DUCK
MOOSE

Words and pictures by Mary Sullivan

HOUGHTON MIFFLIN HARCOURT

BOSTON   NEW YORK

To Arlo, Otis, Hayes, Hart, and Julia.

I love you with all of my heart.

Copyright © 2021 by Mary Sullivan

All rights reserved. For information about permission to reproduce selections from this book, write to trade.permissions@hmhco.com or to Permissions, Houghton Mifflin Harcourt Publishing Company, 3 Park Avenue, 19th Floor, New York, New York 10016.

hmhbooks.com

The illustrations in this book were digitally drawn and colored.
The text was set in Century Schoolbook.
Design by Whitney Leader-Picone and Natalie Fondriest

Library of Congress Cataloging-in-Publication Data is on file.
ISBN: 978-0-358-31349-6

Manufactured in China
SCP 10 9 8 7 6 5 4 3 2 1
4500815376

Up, Duck! Streeeeetch!
Up, Duck! Streeeeetch!
BUZZ
BUZZ
BUZZ
Go, Duck!
Feeeeetch!

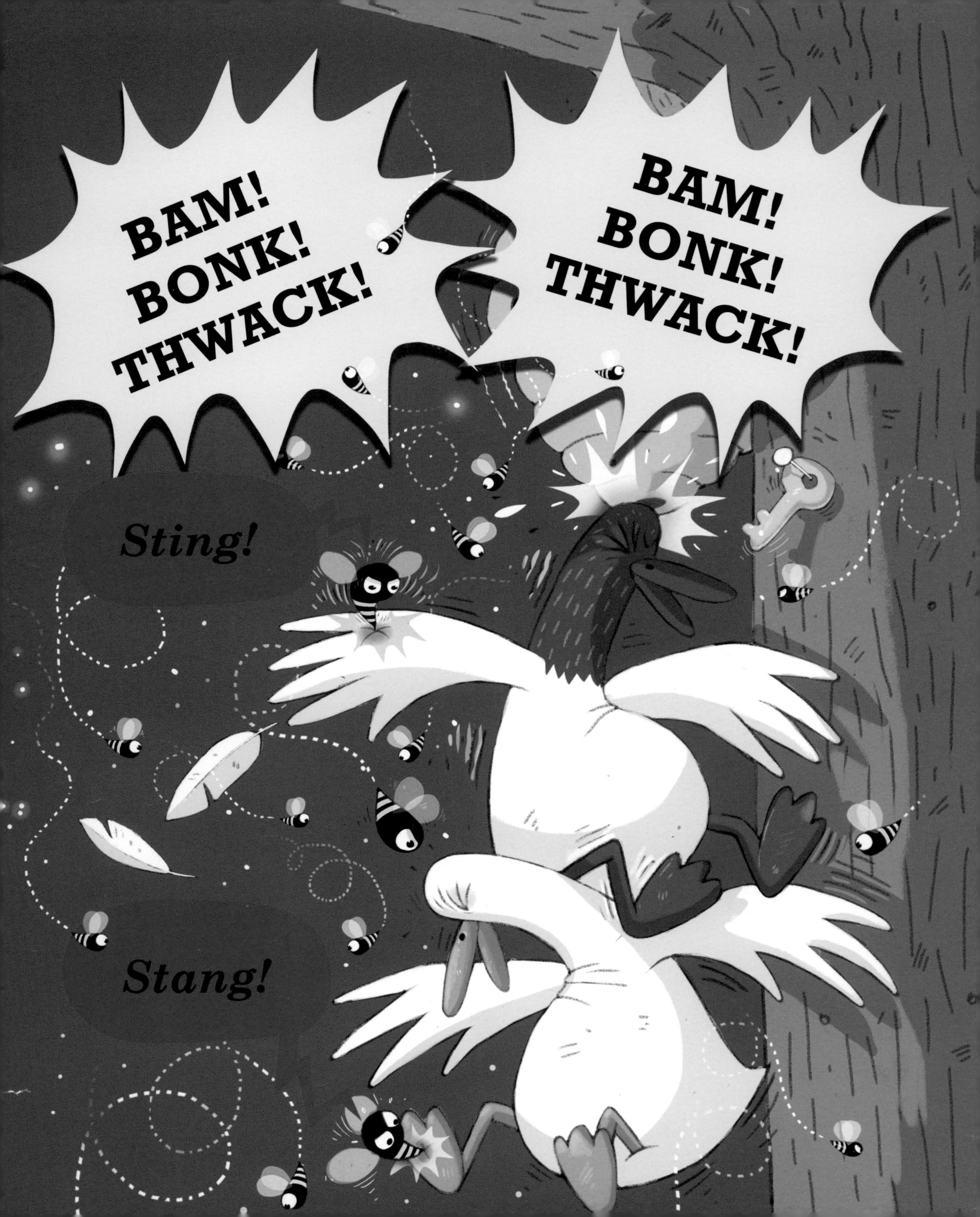
BAM! BONK! THWACK!
BAM! BONK! THWACK!
Sting!
Stang!

Oof!
Grunt!
THUD!

Oof!
Grunt!
THUD!

Down,

down,

down . . .

in the mud.

In Big Moe.

In Big Moe.

Duck,

Duck,

Moose . . .   home they go.

All tucked in.

Day is done.

Time for sleep . . .

everyone.

Mooooooook! Quack! Quack!

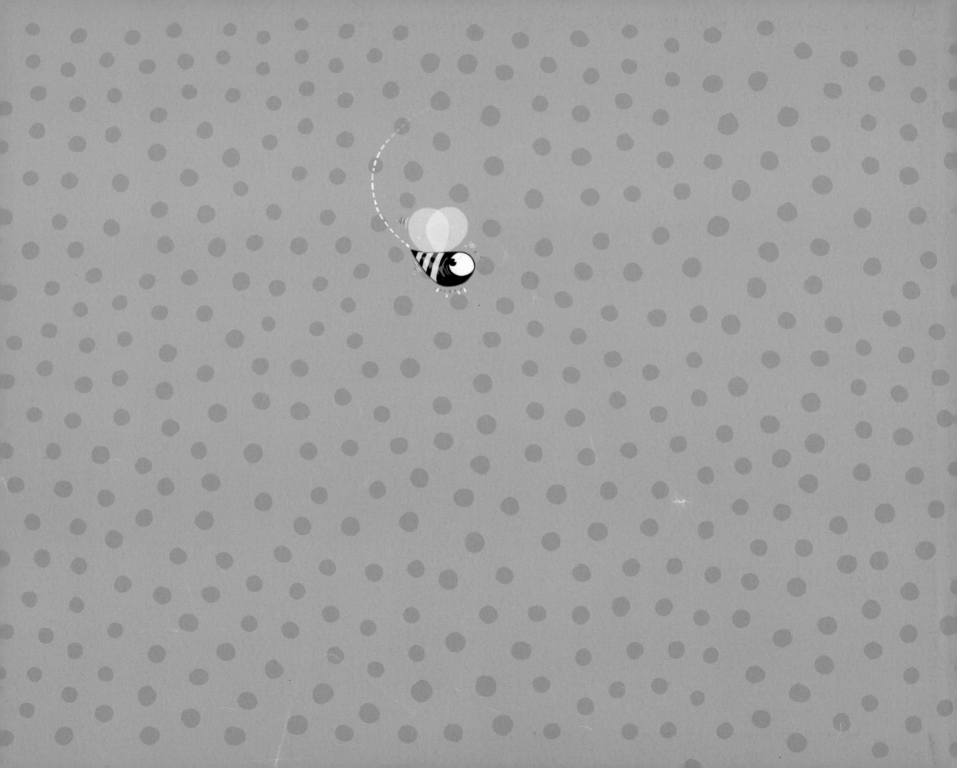